Alone, But Not Lonely:
The Power of Solitude for Strong Women

Gaudelene Joy Dacuan

Ukiyoto Publishing

All global publishing rights are held by

Ukiyoto Publishing

Published in 2023

Content Copyright © Gaudelene Joy Dacuan

ISBN 9789360166021

All rights reserved.
No part of this publication may be reproduced, transmitted, or stored in a retrieval system, in any form by any means, electronic, mechanical, photocopying, recording or otherwise, without the prior permission of the publisher.

The moral rights of the author have been asserted.

This is a work of fiction. Names, characters, businesses, places, events, locales, and incidents are either the products of the author's imagination or used in a fictitious manner. Any resemblance to actual persons, living or dead, or actual events is purely coincidental.

This book is sold subject to the condition that it shall not by way of trade or otherwise, be lent, resold, hired out or otherwise circulated, without the publisher's prior consent, in any form of binding or cover other than that in which it is published.

www.ukiyoto.com

Dedication

"I dedicate this book
to the strongest
and most beautiful woman
I know, my Nanay.
I love you, Nay!"

Contents

Introduction	1
Embracing Solitude	3
The Art of Being Alone	5
The Stigma of Loneliness	10
Self-Discovery and Personal Growth	16
Cultivating Meaningful Relationships	19
Overcoming Challenges and Adversity	23
Alone, But Not Lonely	27
About the Author	*28*

Introduction

The state of being alone referred to as solitude, can have a variety of connotations and be beneficial in several ways. At its most fundamental level, solitude is an opportunity to withdraw from the external world and focus inward on one's identity. It offers a venue for contemplation, reflection, and personal development at any stage of life.

Being alone can be especially beneficial in our modern, always connected, and hectic environment because it allows us to slow down, relieve tension, and recharge ourselves. Because we have the time and space to organize and reflect on our thoughts, feelings, and behaviors, solitude is another way to assess ourselves in developing a heightened sense of self-awareness.

This can help us create a deeper understanding of our identity and enable us to make more informed decisions. In addition, being alone may be a source of creativity and inspiration since it allows us to explore our own thoughts and interests without interfering with other people's perspectives.

Finally, being alone can instill a sense of tranquility and peace, making it easier to connect with our innate intelligence and intuition. Even though being alone might be difficult for some people, it can also be a very effective method for fostering personal development, discovering oneself, and improving one's well-being.

In a world where the urge to conform and fit in can be overpowering, some women prefer to deviate from the norm and embrace their isolation. These women are not alone, but are **strong, independent, and empowered**. They have learned to appreciate the freedom and self-discovery that comes with being alone.

These women have consciously prioritized their mental health and well-being by avoiding toxic relationships, cultural expectations, and external demands. They have found the confidence to embrace their authentic selves and pursue their passions without fear of rejection or condemnation.

While being alone can be frightening, these ladies have learned to overcome their concerns and realize the benefits of solitude. They've used their seclusion to concentrate on their vocations, grow their skills, and achieve remarkable success. They have also discovered methods to connect with people meaningfully, whether through intimate friendships, family relationships, or community activity.

These women serve as role models for all of us, demonstrating that it is possible to prosper without complying with cultural norms. They remind us that our worth and value are determined by our own self-worth and inner power, not by our interactions with others. We can learn who we are, pursue our hobbies, and live authentically by embracing our isolation.

Embracing Solitude

Strong women possess a variety of admirable characteristics that help them navigate through life's challenges with resilience and grace. They are confident in their abilities and are not afraid to take risks to pursue their goals. They are independent and self-sufficient, capable of taking care of themselves and making their own decisions. Strong women are also compassionate and empathetic, showing kindness and support to others in need. They are persistent and determined, never giving up on their dreams despite setbacks and obstacles.

Strong women are also self-aware, recognizing their own strengths and weaknesses and constantly striving for self-improvement. They are not afraid to speak their minds and stand up for what they believe in, even in the face of opposition. Overall, strong women possess a unique combination of strength, resilience, compassion, and determination that makes them a source of inspiration and admiration for others.

Strong women would agree that spending time alone is critical to their overall health and capacity for personal development. They may have a sense of serenity and tranquility and the opportunity to contemplate and replenish their energy while they are alone. It frees individuals from the obligations and stresses of day-to-day existence, enabling them to concentrate on themselves and the requirements of their own lives.

Solitude can be especially significant for powerful women who may be in positions of leadership or responsibility because it gives them the space they require to think, plan, and plot. In addition, strong women who place a high value on isolation are frequently able to cultivate a heightened sense of self-awareness and creativity. They can reflect on their own thoughts, emotions, and interests without being influenced by the perspectives of others when they have time to do so. This can allow individuals to better understand their motivations and aspirations and assess themselves in making decisions in their personal and professional lives that are more informed.

Numerous empowered women have discovered that spending time alone enables them to develop a deeper connection with their intuition and inner wisdom, which may be an essential source of direction and power. Even though some strong women may not enjoy their time alone, most of them understand its value and try to incorporate it into their lives. This may include scheduling regular time independently, attending retreats where they are the only person, or finding moments of solitude amidst their otherwise hectic schedules.

The Art of Being Alone

Strong women can enjoy their alone time in various ways, depending on their hobbies and aspirations in life. Some women might utilize their alone time to experiment with various art forms, be it writing, painting, or music. Yet others may want to work on their bodies with running, zumba, or ballroom dancing. Some people could try gardening, cooking, or even traveling as a new hobby.

Meditation, for instance, is a practice that is becoming increasingly popular because of its potential to alleviate stress and foster a sense of inner quiet and clarity. This makes it an ideal activity for those who want isolation.

Writing in a journal, which may serve as a vehicle for introspection and self-expression, is another way to appreciate the time spent alone. Strong women could also find that traveling alone is enjoyable and a life-changing and powerful experience as they discover new locations and cultures on their own terms.

Those who enjoy engaging in creative activities may find that spending time alone writing a book or participating in another artistic expression can be a satisfying way to pass the time. Hiking in the great outdoors, practicing yoga or one of the many other forms of exercise, or simply spending peaceful time alone with a good book are all examples of different sorts of solitude that powerful women may find beneficial.

Finding activities that are meaningful and fulfilling is ultimately the key to being able to enjoy solitude as a strong woman. Additionally, making a conscious effort to prioritize alone time as part of a healthy and balanced lifestyle is also essential to fully reap from the benefits of solitude.

When women consciously seek out and enjoy their alone time, they give themselves a priceless gift: the chance to deepen their understanding of themselves as individuals, find their hidden abilities, and pursue their passions without distraction. They are free to follow their passions and interests without worrying about what others may think because societal norms and expectations do not burden them.

Women who like their own company can use the time alone to reflect and explore their passions. They can learn more about themselves and what's most important to them by thinking about and analyzing their views, values, and goals. They can take stock of their lives, pinpoint areas where they can make changes, and devise plans to conquer difficulties.

In the end, women who take advantage of their alone time to pursue their interests, develop their skills, and get in touch with their inner selves are giving themselves the tools they need to create a life that is authentic to their values and goals. They are developing self-knowledge and self-assurance to serve them well and encourage others to do the same.

Maya Angelou, a well-known American poet, memoirist, and campaigner for civil rights, is one of many women who have found joy and fulfillment in their solitude.

She acknowledged that she often found inspiration and delight in her alone time. It was common knowledge that she rose before the sun rises to have some quiet time in her garden, where she would write or meditate before beginning her day.

Angelou's affinity for being alone and her deep connection to the natural world are themes throughout most of her writing, including her autobiography "I Know Why the Caged Bird Sings". In this book, Maya Angelou recalled her upbringing in the American South. The book, lauded for its forthrightness and poetic style, delves into topics such as racism, traumatic experiences, and overcoming adversity. Angelou never stopped using her writing to investigate her own life and broader aspects of the human condition. She did this throughout her entire life.

The fact that Angelou enjoyed being alone is reflected in many of her writing, particularly in her poetry. She says in her poetry "Alone" that she was "lying, wondering" the previous night about how to create a place for her "soul" where "water is not thirsty" and "bread loaf is not stone."

The poem contemplates the quest for purpose and connection in a world that sometimes can seem isolated and foreign. For Maya Angelou, being alone was not just a method to discover inspiration but also a chance to connect with the more profound truths inherent in the human experience.

Angelou was well-known not only for her writing but also for her advocacy and activist work throughout her life. She was an outspoken advocate for the Civil Rights Movement and collaborated with prominent personalities such as Martin Luther King Jr. and Malcolm X during that time. She never wavered in her dedication to working for social justice and equality throughout her life, and she effectively used her voice and platform to encourage and enable others. The legacy of Maya Angelou is a testament to the power of isolation and self-reflection as a method of both individual development and societal transformation.

The British novelist and feminist icon **Virginia Woolf**, found comfort in her own company by reading alone. Woolf is most known for her argument that women require "a place of one's own" to write and create without restriction. She spent most of her life writing and pondering in seclusion, frequently withdrawing to a country home where she could be alone with her ideas and get some work done. Woolf's novels, such as "Mrs. Dalloway" and "To the Lighthouse," are well-known for their nuanced studies of the inner lives of women. This was a topic that Woolf could delve extensively into because of her love of solitude.

Her novels are a testament to the power of solitude in creative expression. In the book "Mrs. Dalloway," she delves into the complexity of societal roles and gender expectations by examining the inner thoughts and emotions of a lady getting ready for a party. Similarly, "To the Lighthouse" takes the reader on a journey through her characters' thoughts as they struggle with their aspirations and their interactions with others.

Woolf famously stated, "I need solitude. I need space. I need air. I need the empty fields round me; and my legs pounding along roads; and sleep; and animal existence." Her stream-of-consciousness writing, in which she immerses the reader in the character's thoughts and emotions, is a tribute to the power of solitude in examining the human psyche and is an example of how she capitalized on the strength of isolation.

Woolf's view that women needed the freedom to develop and explore their inner lives to reach full equality with men was the motivation behind her love of isolation. Woolf believed that women needed to be alone to attain true equality with men.

Woolf contends in her seminal work, "A Room of One's Own", that for women to develop their skills and ideas, they want a physical and mental space that is entirely their own and solely dedicated to them. This space was not only a physical chamber for Woolf; it was also a state of mind that required freedom from the restrictions and expectations imposed by the outside world.

Woolf continued to write and create until the awful time she took her own life in 1941. However, she battled various mental health challenges, including anxiety and depression. Her history as a feminist heroine and literary trailblazer is a monument to the power of solitude in allowing women to explore their ideas and find their voices. This is a proof that her legacy is a testament to the power of solitude.

Oprah Winfrey, an American media magnate, and philanthropist, is another prominent figure who has discussed the significance of alone time in her life. Winfrey frequently takes time off herself to recuperate and spend quality time on vacation. In addition, she has mentioned that she begins each morning with some meditation and then proceeds to set her intentions for the upcoming day. Winfrey views isolation as an effective method for fostering personal development and well-being and a source of creative inspiration.

The fact that Oprah Winfrey has been so successful in her various endeavors as a media personality, businesswoman, and philanthropist, demonstrates the significance of time spent alone in pursuing personal and professional happiness. Even though she has a packed agenda,

Oprah has not been shy about sharing her thoughts on the significance of making time for isolation and introspection.

In one of her book, she explains that she believes "solitude is one of the most important things you can have in this world." It is the location where you discover who you are so that you can interact with others from a position of self-sufficiency rather than dependency". Winfrey values her alone time since this is reflected in her daily rituals, which frequently involve time dedicated to meditation and journaling. She has also discussed the importance of solo travel, which enables her to detach herself from the pressures of her job and technology to reestablish a connection with who she is.

During an interview with O Magazine in 2013, she stated, "Time spent by yourself is the best present you can give to yourself, whether it's a little break in the morning or a whole weekend away, the gift of solitude is priceless. So even when you are by yourself, you are never truly alone. You share a connection with something more important than you are."

Winfrey's success as a media mogul and philanthropist has been driven by her capacity to connect with others from a place of self-awareness and honesty. This talent has been the driving force behind her achievements. Her dedication to isolation has allowed her to develop a profound sense of inner wisdom and clarity, which she has utilized to motivate and encourage millions of people worldwide. Finding purpose and meaning in life is essential to Winfrey. For her, solitude is a personal discipline and a means of connecting with something greater than oneself.

The Stigma of Loneliness

A widespread negative stigma is linked to being alone or lonely, particularly for women. This is the case even though there are many positive aspects of isolation. Society frequently portrays women as social beings expected to be loving, compassionate, and permanently surrounded by other people. Because of this, it can be challenging for women to accept their solitude without experiencing embarrassment or isolation. Women who prioritize their alone time or like to be alone can be perceived as being cold, unapproachable, or even weird by other people.

Being alone can be scary, especially when we are bombarded by societal messages that tell us we need others to feel complete. Nonetheless, women need to get over this stigma and learn to cherish their alone time without feeling alienated or embarrassed of themselves.

For women to transcend the negative stigma associated with being alone or feeling lonely, they must acknowledge their need for solitude as both natural and beneficial. Women can also look for other people who share their perspectives and prioritize their time alone, and they can form supportive communities that celebrate the positive aspects of isolation.

Setting up healthy boundaries that enable women to prioritize their time alone without feeling guilty or ashamed is another crucial step for women to take. Women must discuss their needs and limitations with others in their immediate environment.

However, there are some women who have overcome their fear of solitude and found strength in their independence. These women have learned to challenge the societal norms that pressure us to conform and instead, have chosen to embrace their solitude. They have discovered that being alone does not equate to being lonely, and that there is power in their independence. By learning to enjoy their own company, they have developed a deep sense of self-awareness and self-confidence that allows them to navigate life's challenges with resilience and grace.

These women have also found that being alone provides them with a unique opportunity for growth and self-discovery. Without the distractions and influences of others, they can explore their passions, develop new skills, and connect with their inner selves in a way that is not possible when surrounded by others. They have learned to value their alone time as a means of self-care and personal development and have become a source of inspiration for others who may be struggling with the fear of solitude.

The chance for introspection, personal development, and creative inspiration that solitude affords is a priceless asset that can be utilized toward obtaining balance and well-being for oneself. Women who have established a higher sense of inner strength and resilience by embracing their isolation have the potential to develop a more profound understanding of self-awareness and self-worth.

Ultimately, these women have shown us that being alone does not have to be scary or lonely. Instead, it can be a time of empowerment and self-discovery that can lead to a more fulfilling and authentic life.

Hence, we can say that the most essential step in embracing isolation as a strong woman is to realize that it is not a sign of weakness and imperfection but rather a sign of strength and self-love. Women can create a more profound feeling of inner peace, purpose, and fulfillment by embracing the isolation that comes with their lives, and they can inspire other women to do the same.

Eleanor Roosevelt, a former first lady of the United States and the first Chairperson of the Commission on Human Rights, is a well-known example of a woman who triumphed over the social stigma of loneliness and discovered the power of spending time alone.

Roosevelt's husband, President Franklin D. Roosevelt, was required to spend significant time away from home to fulfill his political responsibilities. As a result, Eleanor Roosevelt was left to run the household and raise the couple's children alone. Despite this, Roosevelt sought solace in her solitude and made the most of the time alone by delving deeper into her interests and pursuits. She rose to prominence as an outspoken supporter of human rights and took advantage of her position to rail against various forms of social injustice.

In addition to her advocacy work, Roosevelt produced a significant body of written work detailing her experiences and opinions. Her work continues to motivate and inspire readers all over the world. She has penned various articles and books covering issues ranging from politics to advancing women's rights. Roosevelt stayed unwavering in her beliefs and used her voice to bring about positive change, despite being subjected to opposition and criticism for her viewpoints and activities. She has become an image of female power and leadership for generations of women due to her unwavering dedication to justice and her ability to persevere in adversity.

Alice Walker is a well-known author, poet, and activist from the United States. Walker overcame prejudice and adversity throughout her life due to her upbringing in a rural hamlet in Georgia. Despite these difficulties, she located peace in writing, drawing upon her life for ideas to include in her work and utilizing her voice to advocate for social justice.

Walker's novel "The Color Purple," which was awarded the Pulitzer Prize for Fiction in 1983 and has since become a literary classic that continues to resound with readers worldwide, earned the award for best novel at the time.

Alice Walker is renowned for her activism and writing, but she discovered that being alone provided her with strength and resilience. She discussed the significance of making space for oneself, both physically and emotionally.

In the piece that she titled "In Search of Our Mothers' Gardens", she tells how her mother and other women in her community found consolation in caring for their gardens, using the act of gardening as a method to connect with nature and reflect on their inner lives. She talks of how caring for her garden as a child provided her with a sense of peace and solace. Similarly, Walker could calm her mind and find comfort in the solitude of her garden, where she would spend time writing and meditating. For Walker, being alone was not a cause for embarrassment or alienation; instead, it was an essential component of the creative process and a method to connect with oneself and one's community.

Marlene Dietrich, a German-American actress and singer, was famous for her ferocious individualism and strong sense of herself. Despite her status as a massive Hollywood star, Dietrich was known for frequently withdrawing into seclusion. Between performances, she spent hours alone in the hotel or dressing room she used. Once, she remarked, "I enjoy isolation. That is when you can hear and communicate with the voice that is uniquely your own."

Even though Dietrich was subjected to the tremendous scrutiny and pressure of Hollywood, she was able to keep her sense of who she was and her independence because she enjoyed spending time alone. She has been recognized for her bold dress choices as well as her outspoken political beliefs, and she refused to comply with the traditional gender roles that were expected of women.

Dietrich's later years were marked by an even greater emphasis on her desire for solitude, as evidenced by the fact that she spent her final years in Paris in complete solitary confinement. Despite this, she continued symbolizing strength and resiliency, inspiring generations of women with her ferocious spirit and uncompromising independence.

Icon of feminism and Mexican painter, **Frida Kahlo**, discovered that being alone helped her to grow in strength and resiliency. Most of the time, Kahlo would paint by herself in her studio, allowing her work to be an outlet for her most private ideas and feelings. Although she was plagued by chronic pain and was physically constrained, Kahlo refused to let her isolation bring her down and instead turned to her isolation as a source of motivation and power.

In her artwork, Kahlo frequently depicted herself in a frank and intensely intimate manner, exposing the problems she faced in dealing with her physical and emotional agony. Her paintings were also interwoven with Mexican culture and mythology, creating a singular and powerful artistic vision that recognized her personality and history. Her paintings were a celebration of both aspects of her identity.

Kahlo's ability to find strength and meaning in her solitude has made her an enduring symbol of resilience and empowerment for women worldwide. Even though she faced numerous challenges, such as a troubled marriage and multiple health issues, Kahlo was able to find the strength and meaning she needed in her solitude.

Hedy Lamarr was an actress and an inventor. She was born in Austria. It was common practice to dismiss Hedy Lamarr's interests in science and technology as a vanity project because of her stunning beauty. Despite the stigma, she chose not to let it hold her back and instead put forth a lot of effort to pursue the things she was passionate about.

Lamarr was also well-known for her appreciation of her own company, and she frequently worked on her creations and ideas alone. Lamarr maintained her will and concentration despite her difficulties and disappointments in both her personal and professional life. She utilized the time she spent by herself to make significant contributions to the world.

Her work on radio-controlled missile systems was crucial in laying the foundation for modern Wi-Fi technology. Her legacy as an innovator motivates and enables women in the modern era. Lamarr defied prejudices and paved the way for subsequent generations of women to pursue careers in science and technology thanks to her dogged perseverance and unwavering resiliency.

The narrative of Lamarr serves as a helpful reminder that the stigma of loneliness and the experience of having one's interests or passions disregarded can be conquered with the right amount of perseverance and resiliency. She was determined not to let the demands of society shape who she was, and she pursued her interest in science and technology as well as her fondness for being alone.

Her reputation as an innovator and forerunner encourages other women to defy societal expectations and go after their goals, no matter how unorthodox or complex they may be. The story of Hedy Lamarr is a powerful illustration of the importance of being one's own person and the growth that may occur when one fully embraces their distinctive character and the things that drive them.

These women and many others demonstrate that being alone does not have to be a sign of weakness or a reason to feel ashamed; rather, it can be a source of strength and resilience. They built a more profound sense of self-awareness and inner strength, and they produced works of art and literature that continue to inspire and resonate with audiences today because they embraced the solitude that came with their circumstances.

Self-Discovery and Personal Growth

Solitude can be a powerful tool for self-discovery and personal growth, especially for strong women who are often pulled in multiple directions by their many responsibilities and obligations. Taking time for oneself can provide a much-needed break from the hustle and bustle of daily life, allowing women to reflect on their values, beliefs, and goals and to develop greater self-awareness and self-confidence.

In solitude, women can explore their innermost thoughts and emotions, confront their fears and insecurities, and better understand their strengths and weaknesses. This self-reflection can be transformative, helping women identify their priorities and make important life decisions. By embracing solitude, strong women can cultivate a sense of independence and resilience, empowering them to face the world with greater confidence and purpose.

Some women have also discovered that working alone has benefits rather than drawbacks. They can get more done when they aren't distracted by friends, family, or coworkers. Without distractions, they can focus on their work without worrying about other things.

These women have also demonstrated the benefits of spending time alone, which include the freedom to focus on one's interests without worrying about pleasing others. They've used their time alone to better themselves, learn new things, and follow their passions.

Being alone has thus become a source of grit and empowerment for these women, propelling them toward their goals and helping them to reach their full potential. They've shown us that solitude isn't a death sentence but a path to a more prosperous, more successful existence.

Toni Morrison, an American novelist, editor, and professor found solace in her solitude and used it as an opportunity for deep introspection and self-discovery. Her work often explores themes of identity, race, and trauma, and her writing process was profoundly personal and reflective. She said, "I have to create a space where I can be alone, listen to myself, and not worry about what others are thinking." Morrison's commitment to her voice and perspective allowed her to become one of the most celebrated and influential writers of the 20th century.

The issue of loneliness and its repercussions on women's self-discovery and personal progress is frequently explored in Toni Morrison's works. Throughout her works, she depicts the experiences of Black women who are frequently ignored and oppressed in society, as well as the significance that solitude plays in their road to self-realization.

For Morrison, isolation is more than just being alone; it is a conscious exercise of self-reflection and self-exploration. She contends that women require alone time to connect with their inner selves and comprehend their actual ambitions and objectives.

Sethe, the protagonist in her novel "Beloved," finds seclusion in her cabin, where she is able to dwell on her horrific history and come to terms with her identity as a slave survivor. Sethe is able to grasp her own power and tenacity via this process of self-discovery, and therefore achieve healing and liberation.

Similarly, in "Sula," the protagonist Sula has a moment of solitude while standing on the edge of a cliff when she can confront her own mortality and consider the meaning of her life. Sula is able to accept herself and her decisions as a result of this moment of contemplation, and she eventually finds peace.

Ultimately, Morrison's depiction of loneliness in her writings highlights the necessity of solitude in women's self-discovery and personal progress. Women can connect with their inner selves, confront their anxieties and traumas, and eventually find their own voice and agency in a world that frequently wants to silence them through periods of solitude.

The American journalist and author **Joan Didion** is known for her insightful and introspective writing style. Her work often explores themes of loss, grief, and personal reflection, drawing from her own experiences and emotions. Didion once wrote, "I write entirely to find out what I'm thinking, what I'm looking at, what I see, and what it means." Her time alone allowed her to develop a unique voice and perspective that inspires readers today.

In her works, she emphasizes the importance of finding moments of solitude to reflect on one's life and experiences. Didion's book "The Year of Magical Thinking" is a memoir about her experience of losing her husband and her daughter within a short period of time. Through her writing, she explores the role that solitude played in her journey towards accepting and processing her grief.

Didion argues that solitude is not only necessary for personal growth, but it is also essential for creativity. In her essay "On Keeping a Notebook," she writes about how she uses her notebook as a space for solitude and self-reflection, where she can observe her thoughts and experiences without judgment.

In her novel "Play It as It Lays," the protagonist Maria experiences moments of solitude as she navigates her way through a world that she feels disconnected from. Through these moments of solitude, Maria is able to reflect on her own life and come to a greater understanding of herself and her desires.

Overall, Didion's portrayal of solitude emphasizes its importance in women's self-discovery and personal growth. Through moments of solitude, women are able to reflect on their experiences, understand their own desires and motivations, and ultimately, find a sense of clarity and purpose in their lives.

Women in this chapter not only learned to value their alone time for the benefits it has brought them personally and professionally but have also taken full advantage of the freedom it affords them to follow their passions and realize their goals. They've become leaders in their fields because they make time for solitude and can concentrate on their job without interruptions.

Cultivating Meaningful Relationships

Finding a healthy balance between time spent alone and developing meaningful relationships with other people is essential. However, spending time alone can be an effective method for fostering self-discovery and personal development. Strong women can create more profound and meaningful relationships by being more intentional and present in their interactions with others in their personal and professional lives.

When it comes to relationships, being deliberate involves actively seeking ways to connect with other people, whether through shared interests or experiences or simply by making the time for great talks and experiences together. It also involves engaging in these exchanges with awareness and, in the present moment, concentrating on the activity at hand and the individual in front of you rather than allowing yourself to be drawn away by distractions.

Being present in relationships can also involve cultivating empathetic and compassionate behaviors, such as listening to people without passing judgment and making an effort to comprehend the viewpoints and experiences of others. This can result in more prosperous and meaningful connections and a heightened sense of community and belonging for the individual.

But it is equally essential to acknowledge the significance of time spent alone and to respect the requirement for solitude inside oneself. You can show up in your interactions with other people more comprehensively and genuinely if you practice self-care and care for your health and well-being.

In conclusion, independent women who balance their time spent alone with meaningful connections and interactions can better establish more profound and more gratifying relationships for them. This entails participating in social situations with intention and presence while at the same time attending to one's personal requirements for solitude and taking care of oneself. Finding this balance allows women to build robust and supportive networks of relationships, which can assist them in navigating the obstacles of life and discovering more meaning and purpose in their lives.

Beyoncé Giselle Knowles is an excellent example of a strong woman since she has maintained healthy relationships while still respecting the time she spends alone or in isolation.

Beyoncé, although one of the world's most recognized musicians, has always found time for herself. Whether through meditating, writing, or simply taking vacations from social media, Beyoncé makes sure to take care of herself. She has been able to tap into her inner wisdom and find the courage to overcome the problems she has experienced throughout her life and career by engaging in these practices.

Beyoncé is undoubtedly a very successful musician. At the same time, she has maintained a healthy relationship with her husband, Jay-Z, and they have worked together on several highly successful projects. They have been an influential force in the entertainment business because they have used their music to examine their experiences with love, heartbreak, and personal development.

Beyoncé is also a supporter of women's rights and has used her platform to bring attention to issues like body positivity, gender equality, and racial justice. She has been a champion for women's empowerment for several years.

Beyoncé has maintained equilibrium by recognizing the need to spend time alone or in solitude. This has enabled her to locate the quiet time and space she requires to refuel her energy reserves and think critically. She has been able to deepen her own personal growth and resilience by engaging in this practice, which has also enabled her to build relationships with the people who are most important to her. Her life is an example to women worldwide, reminding us of the importance of taking time alone and practicing self-care on our individual paths toward greater self-actualization and satisfaction.

The life of **Ruth Bader Ginsburg** is a fantastic illustration of a woman who could cultivate meaningful relationships while recognizing the need for her own time spent in solitude or alone. Despite the tremendous demands of her employment and the work she did for advocacy, Ginsburg always made time for the people she loved and her personal ambitions. This equilibrium was unquestionably crucial in assisting her to keep her feet on the ground and remain focused on her work. It also enabled her to keep her resiliency and a sense of purpose despite challenging obstacles.

In addition, Ginsburg's love and support for her husband, Marty, was a compelling illustration of the necessity of these qualities in a healthy relationship. They were married for nearly 50 years, with Marty as one of Ginsburg's closest counselors and champions throughout her career. The couple first met in college and went on to marry. Their commitment to and love for one another served as a source of motivation and motivation for others. It also served as a reminder that healthy relationships are built on a foundation of trust, mutual respect, and a willingness to support one another through the ups and downs of life.

Ginsburg's narrative serves as a potent reminder of how important it is to place a high value on our relationships with those we care about while simultaneously making time for our personal development and well-being. We may strengthen our inner fortitude and resiliency and become better partners, advocates, and contributors to the world that surrounds us if we learn to appreciate the value of solitude and practice self-care.

Michelle Obama's story is another example of a woman who has maintained strong relationships while valuing her alone time or solitude. Despite the demands of her role as First Lady and her advocacy work, Michelle has always been intentional about carving out time for herself and her loved ones. This has been reflected in her commitment to fitness and healthy living and her close relationships with her family and friends.

Michelle's relationship with her husband, Barack, has been a source of strength and inspiration for many. The two have been married for over 31 years and have raised two daughters together. Throughout their time in the public eye, they have been open about their challenges as a couple, including the strains of political life and the demands of raising a family. However, they have also demonstrated a deep commitment and shared values with one another. They have worked together to overcome obstacles and stay connected despite their challenges.

Overall, Michelle's story reminds us of the importance of caring for ourselves and our relationships, even amid busy and demanding lives. By embracing solitude and self-care, we can develop the inner strength and resilience needed to stay grounded and focused on our work while building strong connections with the people we love.

These three women treasured their alone time. They recognized the importance of self-care while maintaining healthy relationships with the people who mattered most in their lives. They balanced their personal and professional lives, setting an excellent example for others.

Overcoming Challenges and Adversity

The concept of overcoming obstacles and difficulties speaks to many women, and the power of isolation is a resource that can assist these women in cultivating resilience, courage, and inner strength.

Strong women have repeatedly demonstrated that they can utilize their alone time to reflect on their experiences, analyze their emotions, and find the fortitude to conquer even the most challenging of challenges. Women can access inner wisdom and draw from internal resources by journaling, meditating, or spending time in nature. This will allow them to find the strength and resilience they need to tackle whatever problems come their way. Women can emerge from challenging experiences stronger, more confident, and better ready to take on whatever comes next if they value the time they spend alone and invest in their well-being. The strength that may be gained from alone serves as a timely reminder that even in the face of challenging circumstances, there is always the possibility for personal development and the development of one's character.

One powerful and resilient woman is **Serena Williams**. Throughout her career, Williams has been subjected to bigotry and racism because she is a Black woman competing in a predominately white sport. She has also triumphed through several physical illnesses and setbacks, including her life-threatening pulmonary embolism in 2011. Despite these obstacles, Williams has proven to be an unstoppable force on the tennis court, where she has won 23 Grand Slam singles titles and established herself as one of the best athletes in history.

Williams is a successful businesswoman, philanthropist, and mother, in addition to her accomplishments on the court as a professional tennis player. She has been a prominent supporter of equal pay for female athletes and has used her platform to speak out against racism and gender discrimination in sports. Williams has also been an outspoken opponent of these issues. Williams has maintained her dedication to using her platform to effect positive change in the world despite the opposition and hostility she has received due to her activism.

The story of Williams serves as a potent reminder that tenacity and dedication may help us triumph over even the most ingrained barriers and challenges. We can make a better world for ourselves and the generations who come after us if we maintain our focus on our objectives, persevere in the face of opposition, and effectively use the platform we have been given to advocate for change. Williams' legacy as one of the best athletes of all time is a monument to her unyielding commitment to perfection, both on and off the court. Her commitment helped Williams earn her place as one of the greatest athletes of all time.

J.K. Rowling is an example of a strong woman who overcomes difficulties and challenges by harnessing the power of solitude. She had to overcome various personal and professional obstacles before becoming a well-known figure, such as numerous challenges in her early writing career, poverty, clinical depression, and being turned down for publication by publishers.

Rowling has been very open about how these difficulties have helped define who she is as a person and as a writer, as well as how they have taught her the necessity of perseverance, resilience, and taking care of oneself. Rowling turned to write as solace and self-expression during this time. She spent hours alone in cafés and coffee shops working on her manuscript and creating the Harry Potter universe.

Despite these obstacles, Rowling never gave up on her dream of being a published author. She could draw into her creativity and imagination through her lonely labor. Her tenacity and dedication were rewarded when she found a publisher for the first Harry Potter novel. The series became a worldwide success, selling over 500 million copies and inspiring a new generation of readers and writers worldwide. Her Harry Potter books brought her the success that she had been seeking.

Nowadays, J. K. Rowling is well-known not only for her writing accomplishments but also for the philanthropic and activist work that she has done. She has utilized her position to speak out on a variety of social problems, including the rights of LGBTQ+ people. She has also been active with various philanthropic organizations, including the Lumos Foundation, which strives to better the lives of disadvantaged children worldwide.

Rowling has used her voice and position throughout her career to campaign for social justice and to speak out against inequality and discrimination. She has also been candid about her mental battles and the necessity of seeking help and support.

The life narrative of J. K. Rowling serves as a potent reminder that success is frequently the consequence of perseverance, fortitude, and the courage to take chances and face hardship. We can overcome even the most difficult challenges and emerge on the other side of them stronger and more resilient if we remain true to ourselves, pursue our passions, and make time for self-care practices.

Ultimately, Rowling's experience demonstrates that, even in the face of significant problems and adversity, the power of solitude may provide strength and perseverance. We can overcome challenges and achieve our goals by tapping into our inner selves and finding solace in our hobbies and pursuits.

Malala Yousafzai is a fantastic example of a strong woman who has surmounted significant hurdles and adversity through her tenacity and grit.

While she was on her way to school in Pakistan in 2012, she was ambushed by the Taliban and shot by one of their members. Malala was forced to undergo rigorous medical care and rehabilitation after surviving a headshot wound. This prompted her to spend a significant amount of time alone and put her resiliency to the test. But despite the horrible experience she had been through, Malala did not allow herself to be silenced and continued to advocate for the education of girls.

Throughout this period, she found comfort in her faith, her family, and her dedication to her cause. Her bravery served as a source of motivation for millions of people worldwide. As a result, she has emerged as a potent symbol of resilience and optimism in the face of tragedy.

Since then, Malala has established the Malala Fund, an organization whose mission is to ensure that all young women have the opportunity to get free, high-quality education for the entire 12 years of compulsory schooling.

Despite persistent threats against her safety, Malala's courage and perseverance have been reflected in her sustained advocacy efforts. She has utilized her voice and platform to raise awareness about the significance of education and human rights and motivate others to take action to make the world a more just and equitable place.

Malala's experiences have demonstrated how solitude can be an excellent weapon for inner strength and perseverance. Despite tremendous obstacles, it can give a space for introspection, healing, and personal growth.

Finally, Malala's experience demonstrates that solitude and self-reflection may provide strength and courage even in the face of adversity. We can connect with our inner selves and discover the resilience and determination to overcome problems and positively affect the world in these moments of solitude.

All these ladies have demonstrated that it is possible to have healthy relationships while respecting one's time spent alone, and it is something that can be done. They have found ways to recharge their batteries and focus on their goals while staying connected to the people who matter the most to them. This can be done through meditation, reading, or spending time in nature, among other activities.

These women's experiences remind us of that perseverance and inner strength may help us triumph over even the most challenging obstacles. We can emerge from adversity more substantial and more resilient than ever if we remain steadfast in our commitment to our aims and ideals, accept our own vulnerabilities, and reach out to others for assistance when we need it.

Alone, But Not Lonely

It is important to remember that being alone does not necessarily indicate loneliness, and solitude can be an excellent method for effectively encouraging self-discovery, personal development, and resilience. In fact, many influential women throughout history have found that spending time alone has been immensely helpful in assisting them in developing their abilities, finding a greater sense of purpose in their lives, and overcoming the challenges they have faced throughout their lives. This is something that they have discovered through spending time alone.

Women can improve their understanding of themselves and the world by devoting some of their spare time to introspection, reflecting on their lives, working through their feelings, and exploring their inner worlds. This can help them develop a better understanding of the world around them. They have the potential to acquire the resiliency and inner fortitude required to overcome challenging circumstances and emerge from them stronger than they were before.

Every woman should cultivate an appreciation for solitude as part of her personal development and self-discovery journey. The experience of being alone can be a powerful force for change. As part of her journey toward personal growth and self-discovery, she should recognize the value of spending time alone. If you ever find yourself in a circumstance in which you are the only person present, you should not be afraid to embrace the power of solitude and use it to help you manage life's challenges with grace and resiliency. You should also be confident to use solitude to help you manage life's problems gracefully and resiliently.

About the Author

Gaudelene Joy N. Dacuan, DLitt, D.Phil

Gaudelene Joy is a recipient of several awards as an educator, dancer, graphic designer, academic and sports coach, and celebrated as an international award-winning author and researcher. She is a public school teacher and a philomath who believes in the beauty of having a little knowledge about everything, and uses it to inspire and empower learners of all ages through her writings.